Where a Bubble Goes

Written by Natalie Hunter
Illustrations by Heather Lenon

I love bubbles!

2

I love to blow them,
chase them,
follow them into trees...

I love to squash them,
pop them, and bounce them
off my knees!

3

But have you ever stopped to wonder,
where a bubble goes?

I've asked all the professionals,
and no one really knows.

You know the bubble that doesn't pop,
the one that gets away?
Well I used to wonder where it went,
until the other day...

I had blown the perfect bubble,
it was shimmery and round!

But when it was supposed to pop,
it bounced right off the ground!

It dashed over the fence,
like it had somewhere to go.

"I have to follow it" I thought,
"or else I'll never know!"

8

As soon as I climbed over,
I couldn't believe what I saw!

Why this wasn't my
neighbor's yard...

It was a bubble carnival!

Elephants and monkeys
were all dancing to the beat,
as the bubble bounced among them,
frolicking between their feet!

"This cannot be real" I thought,
as I was pulled into the crowd!

10

Then we all were **stomping** and **twirling**, and **singing** very loud!

I was having so much fun
that I almost didn't see,

the bubble was bouncing along
again and bopping away from me!

I jumped, and leaped,
then spun around,
and got out of the huddle...

As I finally caught up to it,
it splashed into a puddle!

13

I stopped and then I wondered,
now where did it go?

**"I have to follow it" I thought,
"or else I'll never know!"**

As soon as I dove in,
I couldn't believe my eyes!
Why this wasn't just a puddle...

It was an ocean in disguise!

I was suddenly underwater
and gliding along a reef!

"This cannot be real" I thought,
as I swam in disbelief.

There was an **octopus**, a **sea turtle**, and even an **otter!**

And they all were playing with bubbles miraculously underwater.

17

I raced after my bubble,
as it dove right past my wand!

It started swimming
down,
down,
down
into the deep beyond.

It rolled along the bottom of the
enchanted little sea,
and vanished into a pirate ship that
appeared in front of me!

I stopped and then I wondered,
oh now where did it go?

"I have to follow it" I thought,
"or else I'll never know!"

20

I closed my eyes, swam inside,
and couldn't believe my sight...

I was now back in my yard,
but the day had turned to night.

I scurried up my big oak tree
to see where it had gone.

22

I climbed up to the tippy-top
and gave an exhausted yawn.

23

Then I saw my bubble
twinkling brightly in the sky,

I wanted to keep following it,
but knew this was goodbye.

I laid down on a branch watching
it soar from star to star...

24

"Goodbye my perfect bubble,"
I whispered from afar.

So where does a bubble go,
the one that gets away?

26

It journeys to the most enchanted
places you can imagine in one day.

Like **carnivals**, and **oceans**,
and way up to the **moon...**

And after that, I still don't know.
But I hope to go there soon!

28

SLIPPER and FLIPPER
IN THE
QUEST
FOR THE
GOLDEN SUN

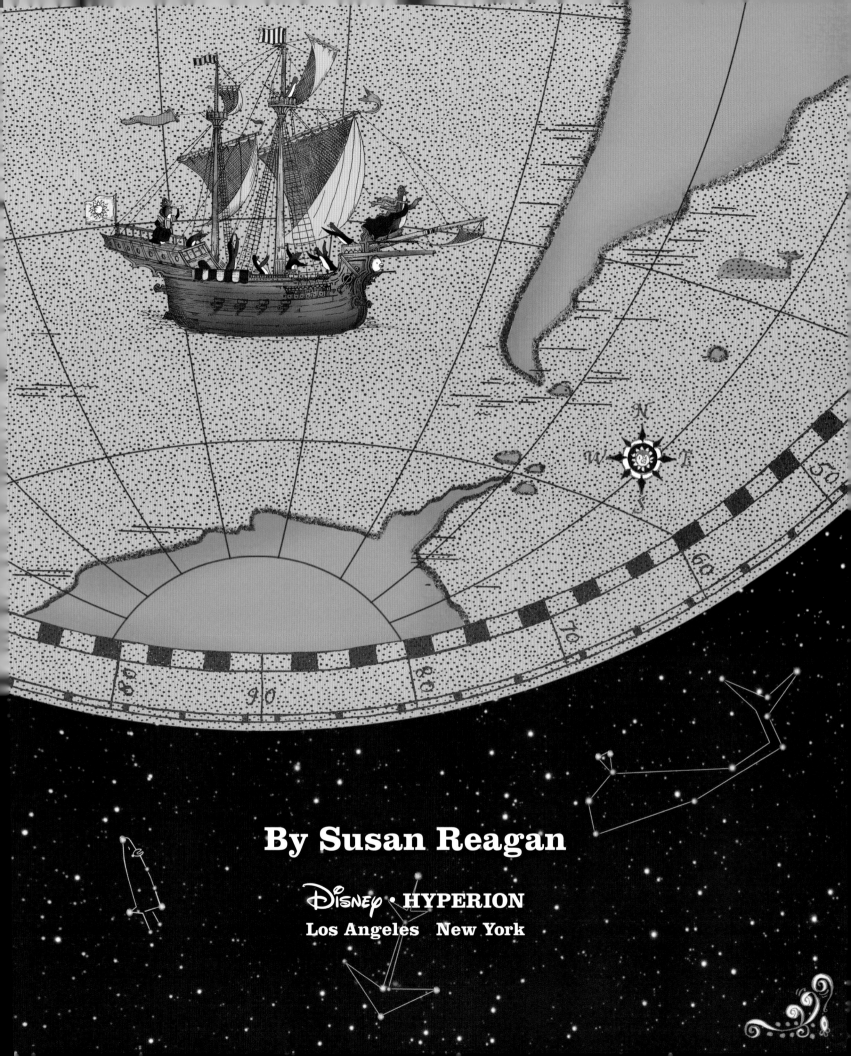

By Susan Reagan

Disney · HYPERION
Los Angeles   New York

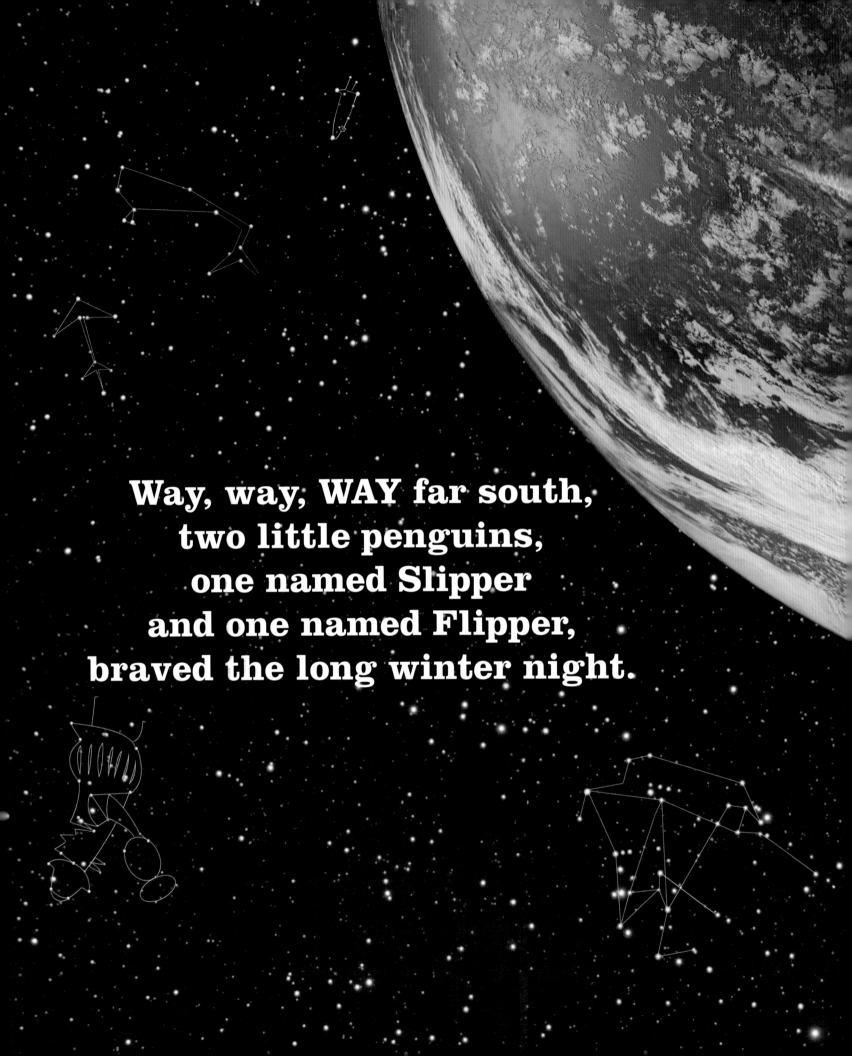

Way, way, WAY far south,
two little penguins,
one named Slipper
and one named Flipper,
braved the long winter night.

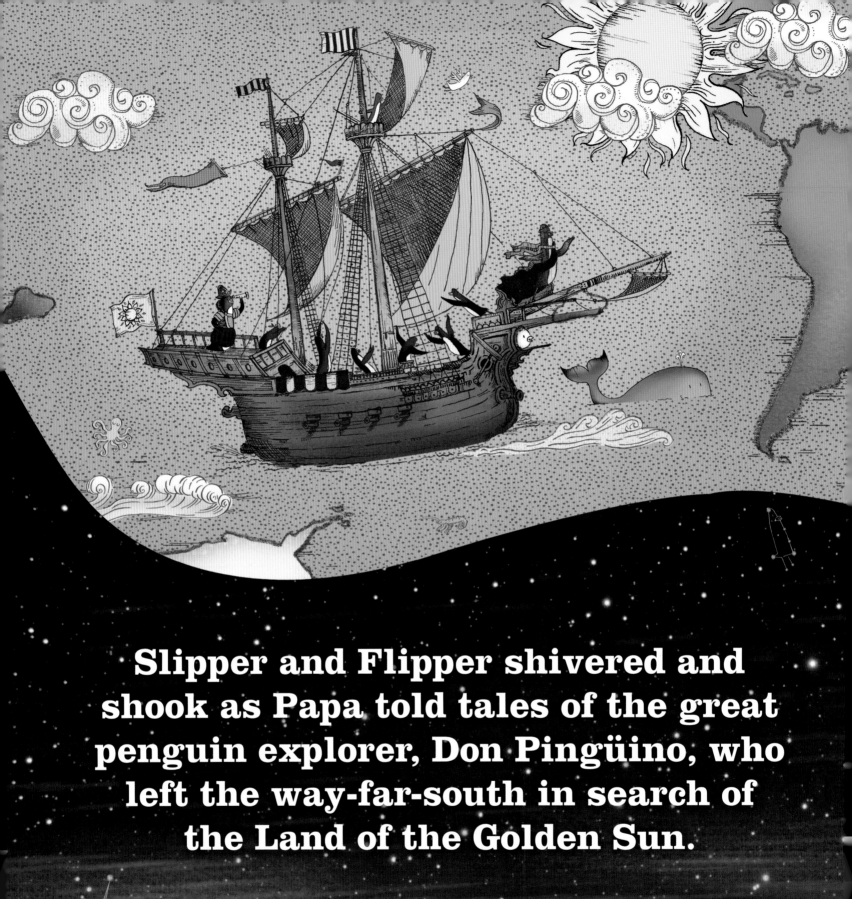

Slipper and Flipper shivered and shook as Papa told tales of the great penguin explorer, Don Pingüino, who left the way-far-south in search of the Land of the Golden Sun.

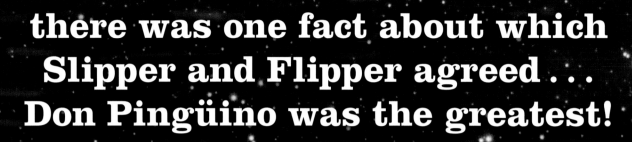

there was one fact about which
Slipper and Flipper agreed . . .
Don Pingüino was the greatest!

until the sun came up and they
set out in search of Don Pingüino
and the Land of the Golden Sun.

Papa didn't worry.
They couldn't go far.

Or so he thought!

Slipper and Flipper drifted and floated and floated and drifted.

Follow those penguins!

On Easter Island, they searched here and there. They searched everywhere.

But no Don Pingüino.

In Buenos Aires they searched here and there. They searched everywhere. But still no Don Pingüino.

In Rio, they searched
here and there.
They searched
everywhere.
But yet again,
no Don Pingüino.

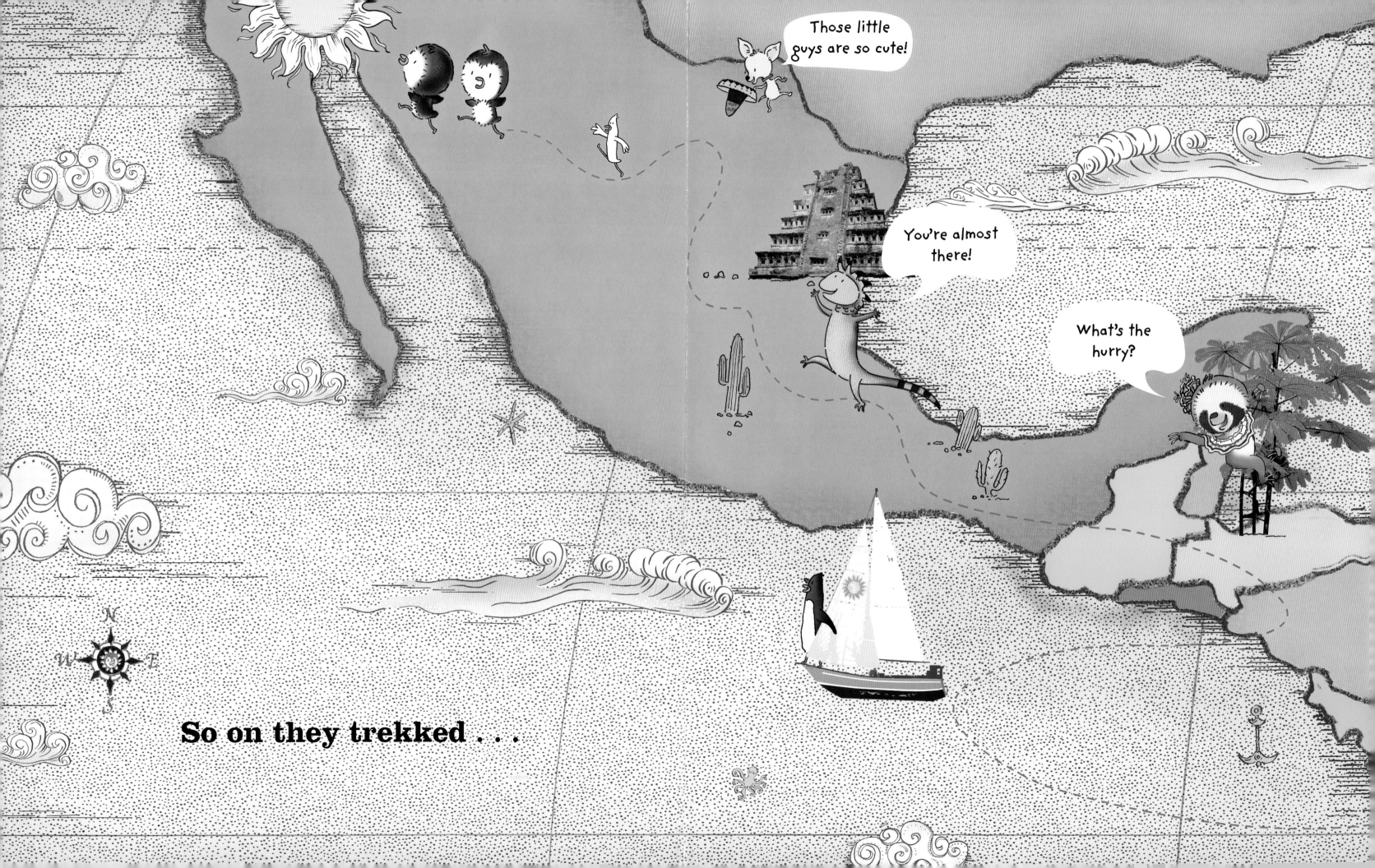

So on they trekked . . .

There, El Abuelo, the oldest of all the villagers, told them of his days with the great Don Pingüino.

♫ Pish pish! Eat fish! Today's a golden day! El Abuelo has met him and did not forget him! Don Pingüino, we're still on our way! ♪

Land of the Golden Sun

Welcome

Bienvenido

We have come in search of Don Pingüino, the great penguin explorer who left the way-far-south in search of the Land of the Golden Sun.

What's this?

Golden Sun Cruises

And they traveled happily ever after.

until they reached the end of their quest!

♫ ♪

Pish pish! Eat fish!
Today is a golden day!
We searched far and near
without any fear!
Don Pingüino . . .

And Papa . . .

♫ ♪ ♪